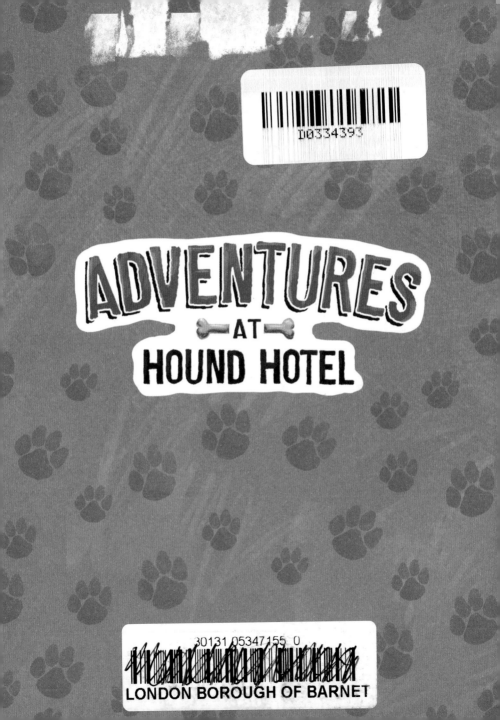

ADVENTURES
AT
HOUND HOTEL

Raintree is an imprint of Capstone Global Library Limited, a company incorporated in
England and Wales having its registered office at 7 Pilgrim Street, London, EC4V 6LB –
Registered company number: 6695582

www.raintree.co.uk
myorders@raintree.co.uk

Edited by Clare Lewis and Julie Gassman
Designed by Russell Griesmer
Original illustrations © Capstone Global Library Limited 2015
Illustrated by Deborah Melmon
Production by Charmaine Whitman
Originated by Capstone Global Library
Printed and bound in China.

ISBN 978-1-4062-9227-5 (paperback)
18 17 16 15 14
10 9 8 7 6 5 4 3 2 1

British Library Cataloguing in Publication Data
A full catalogue record for this book is available from
the British Library.

Growling Gracie

by Shelley Swanson Sateren

illustrated by Deborah Melmon

CONTENTS

ADVENTURES
AT
HOUND HOTEL

IT'S TIME FOR YOUR ADVENTURE AT HOUND HOTEL!

At Hound Hotel, dogs are given the royal treatment. We are a top-notch boarding kennel. When your dog stays with us, we will follow your feeding schedule, take them for walks and tuck them into bed at night.

We are just a short walk away from the dogs — the kennels are located in a heated building at the end of our driveway. Every dog has his or her own kennel, with a bed, blanket and water bowl.

Rest assured ... a stay at the Hound Hotel is like a holiday for your dog. We have a large playground, plenty of toys and a pool for the dogs to play in, in the summer. Your dog will love playing with the other guests.

HOUND HOTEL
WHO'S WHO

WINIFRED WOLFE
Hound Hotel is run by Winifred Wolfe, a lifelong dog lover. Winifred loves all types of dogs. She likes to get to know every breed. When she's not taking care of the canines, she writes books about — that's right — dogs.

ALFIE AND ALFREEDA WOLFE
Winifred's twins help out as much as they can. Whether your dog needs gentle attention or extra playtime, Alfreeda and Alfie provide special services you can't find anywhere else. Your dog will never get bored whilst these two are helping out.

WOLFGANG WOLFE
Winifred's husband helps out at the hotel whenever he can, but he spends most of his time travelling to study packs of wolves. Wolfgang is a real wolf lover — he even named his children after pack leaders, the alpha wolves. Every wolf pack has two alpha wolves: a male wolf and a female wolf, just like the Wolfe family twins.

Next time your family goes on holiday, bring your dog to Hound Hotel.

Your pooch is sure to have a howling good time!

⊷— CHAPTER 1 —⊷
Purple in the race

I'm Alfie Wolfe, and I'm here to tell you all about Gracie the fighting machine. I mean, Gracie the golden retriever.

Yes, she seems nice, calm and quiet when you first meet her. But watch your back. If you turn on her, she'll turn on you! She'll bark and growl and jump up at you teeth-first. She might even draw blood if you're not careful!

Gracie reminds me of my sister. Sometimes Alfreeda acts like Top Fight Picker of the World!

9

She gets really cross when she's tired or unwell or hungry. Then it doesn't matter what I do, everything annoys her. If I don't do everything exactly how she wants me to, she goes crazy.

(Okay, I admit: I can get cross too sometimes. Mainly when I don't get to play enough with the dogs or with my friends.)

Anyway, this story isn't about my sister. Well, not entirely. It's about Gracie – and her little sister, Twinkles the pug.

Their human mum, Doris, calls them her "baby girls." So we call them sisters.

I first met Gracie and Twinkles last year. Last July to be exact. A really busy weekend at our dog hotel to be even more exact.

Our uncle, Robert, brought them over that Saturday morning. You see, the dog's owner, Doris, was Uncle Robert's new girlfriend. We hadn't even met Doris.

The kennels were already fully booked that weekend. Mum, Alfreeda and I had been working like dogs for two days in a row. Our workdays were really long. They started before Spot, our cockerel, even crowed. Then we worked until midnight!

My dad couldn't help in the kennels. He was in Canada again, studying wolves in the wilderness.

Normally, running a dog hotel was lots of fun. But we were so busy, that there was far too much work to do, just looking after those dogs. I couldn't wait to have some actual *fun* with them.

At about nine o'clock that Saturday morning, we were wading through a long list of jobs. Alfreeda was sitting on the floor inside kennel seven.

"Hurry up!" she snapped at me before giving a huge yawn. Her droopy eyes were half closed.

I yawned back at her and walked into kennel seven. I threw a little dog bed onto the floor.

"What took you so long?" she demanded.

I was too tired to argue. I just yawned again and swayed from side to side.

But Alfreeda wouldn't give up. "How did it take you ten minutes to get one tiny dog bed from the storeroom, eh?" she growled at me.

"It wasn't ten minutes!" I said.

"Yes it was!" she snapped. "At this rate, we won't get the jobs finished before next month!"

Her face was turning purple. The veins on the side of her neck stuck out.

Well, I wasn't going to let Alfreeda be the only alpha fighter in our house. (In case you don't know, "alpha" means "first" or "top." In wolf packs, the alpha male and the alpha female are the biggest, cleverest, bravest, strongest and fastest wolves. And yes, they're the most fierce too. They look after the weaker ones.)

I frowned at my sister and shouted, "Stop shouting at me! Mum, Alfreeda won't stop shouting at me!"

"*Shh*," Mum said in a really firm voice. She frowned at us through the wire-mesh fence. She sat on the floor of kennel eight and rocked a homesick dog in her arms. "No fighting today, you two! And I mean it!"

Wow. I couldn't remember the last time Mum had sounded that cross.

She carried on in that cross voice, "I only had about three hours sleep last night, thanks to four homesick dogs. I won't stand for a second of your fighting this morning!"

That put an end to our moaning straight away.

Just then, Uncle Robert's really loud car came roaring up outside. His old sports car made the loudest bangs and backfires you've ever heard. You could hear him coming from a mile away.

"Oh, no," Mum said with a groan. "I've already told him – not today!"

Okay, now that was really strange. Mum always liked it when her brother came over to the hotel. Sometimes he even helped us.

Mum and Uncle Robert had fought like cats and dogs when they were little. But now they're good friends. I'm telling you, that will never happen to my sister and me. Not in a hundred years.

The backfires got louder, which meant his car was right outside the kennel building. "Uncle Robert's here!" Alfreeda and I shouted at the same time.

We jumped up and sprinted towards the

kennel door. We loved Uncle Robert! He gave us sweets and stuff. And he always swung us around in the air really high. It was better than any fair ride!

The race was on for the first swing! Alfreeda and I pushed each other, really hard, in the kennel doorway. We were both trying to blast through first. I won't say who won the pushing match. (Because she always wins. I hate it!)

Alfreeda raced down the hallway and through the office. I sped after her. She threw open the front door and shouted, "Swing me first, Uncle Robert!"

"No, me!" I screamed.

"Oh, are those Doris's dogs, Uncle Robert?" Alfreeda called and leapt off of the front steps.

She ran towards the car. Two dogs hung out of the windows, sniffing all the unfamiliar country smells.

Uncle Robert leaned against his car and grinned at Alfreeda. "Yes," he said. "Meet Gracie and Twinkles. Twinkles is the best Frisbee playing dog I've ever met. Throw a Frisbee high, throw it far – she catches it every single time."

"Cool!" I said and ran towards them. "I want to play with Twinkles!"

"No way!" Alfreeda shouted. "Whoever touches Twinkles first gets to play Frisbee with her first!"

And then she popped her hand right on top of the little pug's head.

CHAPTER 2
Spot goes loopy

About one second later, Alfreeda had taken both dogs out of the car. They already had their leads on.

I leapt over and grabbed the leads right out of her hand.

"Give them back, Alfie!" she said.

Then the dogs snapped the leads right out of my hand. Alfreeda shouldn't have shouted like that! It's all her fault that the dogs ran off.

They ran up our long driveway, all the way

to our house. Then they ran around the house, past the garden, and through the apple trees.

Gracie was in the lead. Twinkles was just behind.

The leads came third, flying behind the dogs.

Gracie and Twinkles ran across the farmyard and started to run around the chicken coop. They ran around it loads of times, so quickly they were almost a blur.

Spot, our cockerel, was going mad. So were the chickens. They flapped their wings and squawked like mad. I'm telling you, it was raining feathers in the farmyard!

Gracie and Twinkles wouldn't stop annoying the hens, and Spot went loopy. He sprang at Twinkles and tried to peck her nose. He missed and tried again.

"Look out, Twinkles!" I shouted. "That cockerel's as big as you are. He could really hurt you. Get out of the way!"

"Don't just stand there shouting, Alfie," Alfreeda said and rolled her eyes. "Do something!"

But she beat me to it. She dashed over and grabbed Twinkles away from Spot.

Alfreeda darted to a tree, not too far from the chicken coop. She searched in her pocket and pulled out a handful of little bone-shaped doggie treats for Twinkles.

Twinkles didn't even wiggle in her arms. She didn't try to get down or anything. Of course not ... not when somebody gives you ten doggie treats instead of one!

"Hey!" I shouted. "Mum says no more than one treat at a time for our guests. Stop trying to win Twinkles away from me!"

"Gracie and Twinkles aren't guests!" Alfreeda shouted back. "They're not paying. They're not staying the night. They're just visiting!"

She had a good point. Anyway, I didn't even have a chance to shout back. That second, Gracie sprang at Spot and took a fierce snap at him.

Uh-oh! Gracie almost had cockerel pie for her mid-morning snack!

Uncle Robert called, "Gracie, here!" He put his fingers in his mouth and whistled.

But Gracie got even more fierce with Spot. She nipped his skinny yellow legs and then his flapping brown feathers. To be honest, I'm not that keen on grumpy old Spot. But I didn't want him to die.

I clapped my hands and shouted, "Gracie, here!"

But she just wouldn't stop!

Then Alfreeda marched up to Gracie, with Twinkles still in her arms. She leaned in so closely that Twinkles got a little slap from Spot's wing.

"Stop, Gracie," Alfreeda said. "Come."

Well, I couldn't believe my eyeballs. Gracie backed away from Spot and stood next to Alfreeda. Spot backed away too.

Gracie panted and stared at my sister, waiting for her next command.

Alfreeda took Gracie's lead and led her to Uncle Robert. Gracie didn't try to break free or anything.

Alfreeda handed the lead to Uncle Robert. She dug in her pocket and gave Gracie a whole handful of dog treats, too. About twenty!

That's when I noticed: Alfreeda's jean pockets were stuffed with dog treats. She must have smelled like a doggie-treat factory. Of course Gracie and Twinkles were following her around without a fight.

"Wow!" Uncle Robert did a long, slow whistle. He gave Alfreeda a high five.

"Whenever Doris is away, you can be the dogs' new pack leader!"

I thought, *What? Can't he see that her pockets are full of dog treats? It's a trick!*

I was so cross, I couldn't speak.

Alfreeda said thank you and bowed. Then she jumped back up and took another bow.

Suddenly I felt like I might go loopy, too! "Hey!" I shouted at her.

She looked at me. "What, Alfie?" she asked in her tired-teacher voice.

"Give me Twinkles," I demanded.

"No," she said. "I'm taking her to the playground. We're going to play a killer game of Frisbee —"

"Oh, no you're not," Mum interrupted her.

We all spun around. Mum stood on the front steps of the kennel building. Her hands were on her hips.

"Robert," she said in a firm voice. "Take those dogs back to Doris's house. Now."

"Oh, come on. Let them stay," Uncle Robert begged. "I can't look after Gracie for a whole day. She hates me! She's going to draw blood one day!"

"Don't be silly," Mum said. "I'm sure Gracie's a perfectly gentle dog most of the time. We're just too busy to take on one more dog, let alone two."

Well, I couldn't just stand there and watch the best Frisbee dog in the world get away. I had to play Frisbee with Twinkles! I sprinted across the driveway, leapt onto the steps, and grabbed Mum's hands.

I wrapped her fingers tightly around mine. Then I held them against my heart.

"Mummy?" I said, just like I used to when I was a little boy. That always used to make Mum give in when I wanted something. I'd just say "Mummy" instead of "Mum."

"Please, Mummy," I begged. "Let Twinkles stay. I've been working and working. Can't I play Frisbee with her, just for five little minutes? Oh *pleeeease*, Mummy?"

Mum stared at me.

I was expecting a big smile, a cuddle and a *yes*.

CHAPTER 3

Calm down, Alf

That's when Mum completely lost her rag.

She dropped my hands and screamed, "I don't have time for this! I'm *sooo* busy! And I'm *sooo* tired!"

She marched around me and down the steps. She headed straight for Uncle Robert.

Mum stopped right in front of him and put her nose up to his. "N. O." You know Mum is serious when she spells her answers.

"Please, Winifred?" he begged. "*You* don't

have to look after Twinkles or the monster, I mean, Gracie. Let the twins look after them!"

"Robert!" Mum cried. "You don't understand! They can't look after Doris's dogs because I need their help! Eleven dogs need walks, water, baths, brushing, feeding and comforting! Perhaps the kids can play after dinner, but they cannot play now!"

"Not until after dinner?" Alfreeda and I cried at the same time. "Please, Mum!"

She didn't even answer us.

"And honestly, I can't look after Gracie today, Robert," Mum was almost shouting now. "I just can't handle another fighter today! So stop trying to get out of doing your job. Doris expects *you* to dogsit on Saturdays when she's working, not me!"

Mum had started to wave her arms around

in the air, like a windmill. Her face had turned sort of purple. The veins on her neck stuck out.

It was real scary, seeing my own mother like that.

Uncle Robert stepped forwards. Now his nose actually touched Mum's.

I thought, *Uh-oh, here comes war.*

"Winifred?" he said.

"Yes?" she snapped and frowned at him.

"You," he said, "need a nap."

Suddenly Mum stopped frowning. She sighed and her stiff shoulders relaxed.

"Actually," she said in a quiet voice, "that is exactly what I need."

"I know," he said and patted her shoulder.

"Let me guess. You're overworked. You haven't had enough sleep."

Mum nodded.

"Go," he said. "Sleep for a few hours. I'll finish off all of the hotel jobs. The twins can play with Twinkles and the monster, I mean, Gracie."

"Really?" Mum asked.

"Absolutely," he said.

Wow! I couldn't imagine ever doing something that nice for my sister. Not in a thousand years.

Then Uncle Robert hugged Mum. She hugged him back.

I thought, *That would never happen between Alfreeda and me. Not in a MILLION years!*

"Thank you, Robbie." Mum said. She ran into the house.

The rest of us walked to the kennel building. Gracie and Twinkles led the way. Uncle Robert held their leads and walked in front of Alfreeda and me.

We didn't even get to the office before she started to argue with me again.

All I'd said was, "Follow me, Twinkles. The Frisbees are in the storeroom."

Alfreeda shouted, "No way!"

Uncle Robert spun around and stopped. We bumped into him and immediately stopped arguing.

He held up his hands. "Okay," he said. "It seems as though you two are tired too. And let me guess. You're not getting enough time to play."

We nodded.

"We'll find a way to fix that," he said. "But first, how about drawing straws to decide?"

"We don't have any straws," Alfreeda said.

"Okay then, pencils," Uncle Robert said and grabbed two off the desk. He grabbed them so quickly, I didn't see how long they were. He held the ends in his fist. Our uncle has big hands, and all I could see were the dog-shaped rubbers sticking out of the top.

"Draw," he said. "Whoever gets the longest pencil gets to play with Twinkles first."

"That's not fair!" I cried.

"She always wins! Even in a game of chance, she always beats me!"

Alfreeda grabbed a pencil before I even had chance to think. She shrieked and cried, "Woo-hoo! I've got the longest! It's not even sharpened!"

"See, Uncle Robert?" I frowned. "She always wins. At everything. Just because she was born five minutes before me, she acts as though she's the only alpha child in this house! I can't stand it anymore!"

"Alfie," said Uncle Robert, patting my shoulder. "Slow down. Take a deep breath."

I did.

"Another," he said.

I did. Actually, the extra air made my head feel a little less like exploding.

"Now draw," he said. So I did. I looked at my pencil and laughed. "It's not sharpened either," I said.

"That's right," said Uncle Robert. "It's a tie. You'll each get to play with Twinkles for thirty minutes. The other will play with Gracie for that half an hour." He took off his watch and gave it to Alfreeda. "Take turns all day if you like."

"Hey!" I said. "Why does she get to wear your watch?"

"Because you, Alf, get to play Frisbee with Twinkles first," he said and handed Twinkles' lead to me.

"Cool!" I said.

"No!" Alfreeda cried. "Why him?"

"Because," Uncle Robert said in that same old laid-back voice, "you're the only one Gracie will listen to! You're top dog in her eyes. That's pretty cool, isn't it?"

"Suppose so." Alfreeda's frown turned to a grin. She took Gracie's lead. "Come on, Gracie, let's go and play catch together." She led Gracie down the hallway towards the playground gate.

I couldn't believe my uncle. He was blasting bad moods to pieces all over the place.

"Okay, Alf," he said to me. "I'm taking the other dogs for a nice long walk."

"All eleven of them?" I asked and laughed.

"Why not?" Uncle Robert grinned and shrugged. "It's a big wide country lane out there, Alfie."

"It certainly is," I said and grinned back at him. "Come on, Twink, old girl."

And we ran to the storeroom to get a Frisbee.

⊶ CHAPTER 4 ⊷
Tug-of-beak

Twinkles and I sprinted from the storeroom to the playground.

"Come on, Twink," I called. "Follow me."

Our grassy playground is massive, so I led her far away from Gracie and Alfreeda. They were playing catch on the chicken-coop side of the park.

Twinkles barked excitedly and ran next to me. She didn't take her big round eyeballs off the Frisbee in my hand. Not for one second.

Finally, I stopped and waved it in front of her nose. "Here it goes!" I shouted.

I threw the Frisbee backhand. It flew across the park. Twinkles shot towards it, then she jumped! She flew about two feet up in the air — and then she caught it!

"Wow!" I cried. "That was amazing, Twink!"

She trotted up to me with the Frisbee in her mouth and dropped it at my feet. She went, "Woof!" I knew exactly what she was saying: *Throw it again, Alf! Hurry up, Mr! Throw it higher!*

"No problem," I said. "Catch this if you can."

I took a run up and launched the Frisbee as hard as I could. Twinkles tore after it and jumped even higher this time!

But she missed the Frisbee. It got caught

in the wind and flew over her head. It soared towards the bright blue sky and sailed right over the fence.

It landed in the field of grass on the other side.

Twinkles looked at me and barked.

"No problem," I said. "I'll go and get it."

But Mum had the key to the gate on her key chain. She always kept the gate locked. So I climbed up the fence and sat on top of it, ready to jump.

Suddenly I froze. Two chickens darted over and started to fight for the Frisbee. For some strange reason, they both really wanted it. I'm telling you, it was like they were playing tug-of-beak!

Then Gracie shot to the fence. She stood

below me and started to bark her head off at the chickens.

Next, Spot flew over. He started to flap his wings and squawk at Gracie!

And what do you think Gracie did? She growled at Spot and clawed at the fence, trying to get to him for a tasty cockerel feast.

Gosh, I had to hang on tight. All the fighting made the fence jerk from side to side!

Gracie stuck her nose through a hole in the fence, trying to get even closer to her prey. Spot didn't waste a second. His neck feathers puffed right out, preparing himself for battle.

Then he pecked Gracie on the nose.

Did Gracie back down? No!

"Gracie, here!" Alfreeda shouted. "Spot's really going to hurt you! Here!" My sister even stamped her foot.

But Gracie kept growling and clawing and sticking her nose through holes in the fence. And Spot kept pecking at her nose. It must have hurt!

In a flash, Alfreeda leapt over and grabbed Gracie's lead. My sister pulled the lead like a Saint Bernard hauling an injured skier up a steep mountain.

She dragged Gracie away from the fence. But then, Gracie dug her paws into the earth and yanked the lead.

Alfreeda flew through the air like a human Frisbee. She soared for about three metres, then landed with a thud in a pile of mud. She didn't let go of the lead throughout the whole thing! It was actually quite impressive.

"Yow!" she cried.

Gracie dragged her a bit further until Alfreeda let go of the lead.

I leapt off of the fence and sprinted towards my groaning sister.

❧— CHAPTER 5 —❧
Cockerel stew and roasted boy

At alpha-boy speed, I trapped the monster, I mean, Gracie, in kennel number seven. Twinkles, too.

It wasn't easy though – it took all of my muscles to get both dogs inside.

Alfreeda didn't help at all. She just dragged her feet into the kennel kitchen, really slowly. Her knees didn't even bend. She walked really stiffly and left the whole thing to me.

I wiped my sweaty face with my sweaty Hound Hotel T-shirt. Then I stared through the kennel at Gracie and shook my head. Uncle Robert had been right. Gracie was a fighting machine.

She paced backwards and forwards, checking me out. I knew exactly what she was thinking: *Bring me some cockerel stew. Or maybe a roasted boy. I don't care which one, just bring me some MEAT!*

Twinkles lay on the little dog bed in kennel seven. She panted heavily.

"Hang on, Twink," I said. "I'll get you some water."

I went to the storeroom, grabbed a small water bowl and walked through to the kitchen sink. Alfreeda was sitting at the table in the kitchen, trying to open the first-aid kit. She was only using her left hand.

I noticed the palm and fingers on her right hand were scratched all over and covered in blood. So were her knees.

She looked pretty helpless. She couldn't even open the box with one hand. If you ask me, it shouldn't have been that hard. I almost laughed.

But I didn't. Instead, I remembered the time when I was little.

I'd fallen off a slide at a park in town and hurt my wrist quite badly. It was so sore, I couldn't even put my socks on by myself for about three days.

Alfreeda just kept trying to lift the latch with her left thumb and pointing finger. She just grunted and carried on trying to push the box open.

Suddenly the box shot off of the table. It sailed through the air like a fat metal Frisbee and landed on the floor with an enormous bang. The noise made her jump.

I didn't even laugh at that, which really surprised me. I just picked up the box and put it on the table. Then I opened it for her.

She took out a plaster. She pulled the wrapping off with her teeth. Then she tried to stick the plaster on her right palm with her left hand.

Well, the sticky ends got stuck to her fingers. She shook her hand, trying to get the plaster off.

It came off, all right. It shot like a skinny Frisbee over the table and stuck to the wall. Alfreeda sighed and stared at her sore hand.

I grabbed the box and dug through it. I took seven plasters out. I worked out that she'd need at least that many to cover all of her scratches and scrapes.

I opened them all and laid them sticky-side-up on the table.

Alfreeda stared at me.

"What are you looking at?" I asked.

"Uh, thanks, Alfie," she said in a quiet voice.

"No problem," I said and shrugged.

But for some really strange reason – don't

ask me why – I didn't stop there. I grabbed one of the open plasters.

"Hold your hand out," I said. I covered up some of the scratches. I put another one on her hand, then five on her knees. The right knee looked worse than the left. But they both looked quite sore, if you ask me.

"Thanks, Alfie," she said. And that's all she said.

I just shrugged.

I filled Twinkles's water bowl and made my way back to kennel seven. Gracie saw me coming and did a low slow growl.

"Calm down," I ordered her. "This water is for Twinkles. I'll get you some in a minute, if you're nice."

I squeezed through the gate and put the dish in front of Twinkles. But straight away, Gracie pushed Twinkles aside and drank all of the water herself.

"Hey!" I said. "That wasn't for you! Can't you see how thirsty Twinkles is?"

I frowned at Gracie and grabbed the bowl. Then in my firmest army-command voice, I said, "Gracie, I'm going to get some more water, do you understand? For Twinkles. And you're *not* going to take a single sip of it, do you hear me?"

My voice had started to get really loud. I noticed that my arms had started to wave around like a windmill. (My face may have been purple and the veins on my neck could have been sticking out, but I couldn't see – I didn't have a mirror.)

I turned around and reached towards the gate latch. Suddenly I heard a *whoosh* behind me.

I looked over my shoulder and saw Gracie

flying straight at me like a huge furry Frisbee.
Her mouth was wide open, and I saw a lot of
pointy, sharp-looking teeth.

They locked onto my bottom. "*Yow!*" I
screamed.

CHAPTER 6
This is my territory, Mr

I screamed and jumped sideways. I somehow managed to pull my bottom away from Gracie's teeth.

At alpha-boy speed, I scaled the kennel's fence. I jumped into kennel eight and stood there for a minute, panting heavily. And rubbing my sore bottom.

Okay, so it didn't really hurt much. Actually, it didn't hurt at all. Gracie hadn't torn my jeans or anything.

But still. I'm sure she could've drawn blood.

To be honest, I knew an interesting fact about golden retrievers: they've got soft mouths. They can carry things around in their mouths and not hurt them, not even small live animals.

Still, she did have lots of big teeth. Perhaps that was my warning. Perhaps next time, it would be bruises and blood puddles.

"Look, Gracie," I demanded. "you've got to let me into your kennel, and no more attacks, okay? Twinkles. Needs. Water."

Gracie just eyeballed me. She sat down in front of her little sister.

Well, I knew what she was doing. Not to brag, but I know a lot about dogs and wolves, how they operate in packs and things like that. My dad has taught me all sorts of stuff. It was easy to read Gracie's mind.

I was pretty sure she was thinking: *This kennel is MY territory, Mr. I'm the leader of this pack. And you're not a member of it. So go away before I bite your bottom again.*

The thing is, I couldn't blame her. She was just acting like her natural-born self. You see, every dog's great-great-great (add a lot more greats here) grandparents were wolves. Even after so many great-great grandparents, dogs are still part wolf. I mean, all dogs. Even little pugs and big retrievers.

Dogs think their human families are their packs. Every pack has a leader, and often it's not the human who's in charge. Quite often, the dog takes on the job of caring for the whole pack.

So if a dog like Gracie decides that she's the alpha wolf, then she has to be fierce. It's her job to keep the weaker wolves safe by fighting off enemies. In the wild, different wolf packs are enemies. Wolf packs stay well away from each other. If another pack comes close, it usually spells danger.

Well, standing there in kennel eight, I'd worked it out: in Gracie's mind, she belonged to a pack with three members – Doris, Twinkles and herself. In her mind, Uncle Robert belonged to another pack. And so did I.

To Gracie, Uncle Robert and I smelt like danger. So she had to put us in our place.

I peered through the fence at her.

"Gracie?" I said. "You're a clever dog. But guess what? You need to watch out. Because I'm about to outsmart you."

I marched out of kennel eight and made my way towards the storeroom.

🐾 🐾 🐾

In no time, I came marching back with a big Hound Hotel doggie pillow tied onto my bottom.

I'd wrapped a lead around my stomach about five times. I'd tied a double knot, too. That pillow wasn't going anywhere.

I opened the gate to kennel seven and marched in.

"Hello there, Gracie Old Girl," I said in my coolest alpha-boy voice. I stepped over her and grabbed Twinkles's water bowl. Then I spun around, cool as a frozen doggie treat and marched back to the kennel door.

Suddenly I heard a *whoosh* behind me. I felt a hard yank on my pillow armour.

I looked back over my shoulder. Gracie had about half the pillow inside her mouth! I'm not joking!

She started to growl and tug my pillow armour from side to side. Gracie pulled me forwards and backwards, and she even spun me all the way around – twice!

On the third spin, I dived towards the fence. Somehow I managed to grab it. With all of the alpha-boy power I could muster, I began to scale that fence.

It was no good. I couldn't even climb a metre off of the ground. Gracie had the strength of a female alpha wolf in the wilderness.

I hung on tight to the fence, even though Gracie kept tugging me from left to right, right to left. It was getting harder to hang on. My fingers were killing me!

But I couldn't let go. Or Gracie would pull me to the floor. That's the last place I wanted to be.

"Alfreeda!" I screamed. "Help!"

She came to the doorway and just stood there. She stared at me and wrinkled up her face. "You're so strange, Alfie Wolfe," she said.

I screamed with all of my alpha-boy lung power, "Do something!"

CHAPTER 7
It's your fault, Alfie

Alfreeda really took her time coming to my rescue. She moved so slowly across the kennel, her knees still stiff. Maybe she was still in pain from being dragged along by Gracie earlier.

Eventually, she made it into kennel seven. She grabbed Gracie's collar and pulled her away from me.

"Sit," Alfreeda commanded.

Gracie sat.

Alfreeda began to dig the contents of the pillow out of Gracie's mouth. Then she went nose-to-nose with her.

"Listen, silly," she said. "We don't eat Hound Hotel pillows. We lay our sleepy heads down on them and have sweet dreams, okay?"

Gracie barked.

"Good," Alfreeda said to her. "Glad you understand. Now, stay."

Gracie stayed.

Alfreeda dug some dog treats out of her pocket. She laid them on the floor, and Gracie started to gobble them up.

Then slowly and stiffly, Alfreeda walked over to the rubbish bin on the other side of the kennel. She threw the pillow stuffing into the bin.

I was still hanging onto the fence. My face was

pressed against it. I didn't dare move a single muscle.

Alfreeda came back, then nice and slowly, I put my feet onto the floor and turned around. I leaned on the fence and didn't move.

But straight away, I realized I didn't need to worry anymore. Alfreeda had yawned and sprawled out across the kennel floor. And Gracie had flopped down next to her.

Alfreeda put her head on Gracie's stomach and closed her eyes. Gracie closed her eyes too. They both seemed tired of fighting and everything else.

Then Gracie started to breathe slowly and deeply. The fighting machine was fast asleep!

"Hey," I whispered. "Why did she attack me but not you? You're not part of her normal pack. I can't work it out. It can't just be the treats."

"*Shh*," Alfreeda said. Her eyes were growing really heavy. I suppose that being thrown through the air had really worn her out. "It's your fault, Alfie. You must have forgotten – you never turn your back on a dog that doesn't like you."

"I didn't," I said.

"Yes you did."

"Prove it," I demanded.

"The proof is in the pillow," she said and yawned. "You, Alf, must have turned your back on Gracie. How else could she tear apart a pillow that was tied to your bottom?"

She had a good point.

"Perhaps you didn't notice," Alfreeda added in a sleepy whisper, "but I backed out of the kennel when I went to the rubbish bin just now. I backed out, giving her a huge smile, because —"

"Because," I interrupted her, "dogs are as afraid of our teeth as we are of theirs. And they're afraid of teeth and beaks on other animals, too. Yeah, yeah, I know."

"Exactly," Alfreeda whispered. Her eyes were almost closed now. "And that's why Gracie didn't bite Spot. Because Spot didn't turn his back on her. Dog attacks always happen from behind, because that's the side that doesn't have teeth. Or a beak…"

I almost shouted, *Stop telling me things I already know! I just forgot, okay? Give me a break!*

But I didn't. Because my sister's eyes were completely closed now. And anyway, I'd worked something out, after watching Uncle Robert in action: keeping your cool when somebody tries to start a fight with you is like pouring a bucket of ice on a fire. If you keep cool and be nice, the other person will calm down.

Actually, alpha wolves are really good at that. Sometimes, beta wolves start fights with the leader. ("Beta" means "second," as in "second in command.") The alpha always keeps its cool and the beta backs off.

I looked over at Twinkles. There she was, still lying on the little dog bed. She looked thirsty, and I think she was craving some Frisbee time. I tiptoed over and whispered in her ear, "Hey, Twink. Let's go and have some fun. But be really quiet, okay?"

She jumped up and bobbed her head. Together, we tiptoed out of the kennel door.

Suddenly Alfreeda said, "Gracie, you're a really bony pillow!"

I stopped and spun around. Alfreeda was wiggling around, trying to get comfortable on Gracie's ribs.

If my sister noticed that I was taking Twinkles out for some Frisbee, she would get up and try to take him away from me. I somehow had to get my sister to fall asleep and stay asleep. It was my only hope for extra time with Twinkles.

And I knew exactly what to do.

I whispered in Twink's ear, "*Shh*. Be really quiet, pal. I'll be back in a second."

CHAPTER 8
Frisbee land!

I dashed to the storeroom and ran straight back. I had a pile of Hound Hotel pillows and blankets in my arms.

I tiptoed into kennel seven and whispered, "*Shh*," to Twinkles. Then I tapped Alfreeda on the shoulder.

She opened her eyes halfway and blinked slowly at me. "What is it?" she whispered.

"Here," I whispered back. "No more bony pillow. Take these."

I even helped her spread out the blankets and make a nice cozy bed.

"Uh, thanks, Alf," she said and looked at me, really surprised.

"No problem," I whispered and shrugged.

She put her head down on a comfy doggie pillow. In seconds, she was fast asleep. She started to snore like a pig. Yes!

"Come on, Twink," I whispered. We tiptoed out of the kennel.

Seconds later, we were in the park, with the kennel building's door shut firmly behind us.

"Here we are!" I cried. "Right smack in the middle of Frisbee Land! First, let's get you a some water, okay Twinkles?"

I quickly ran and got her some water from the hose. Then I grabbed the Frisbee.

With a flick of my wrist, it flew across the field.

"Get it, girl!" I shouted.

Twinkles bolted across the park. She flew through the air – and caught the Frisbee! She dashed back and dropped it at my feet. She barked like mad. It was so easy to read her mind: *Hurry up, Alf! Throw it again!*

So I did.

"Go, Twink!" I threw the Frisbee across the park again. Not too high. Not too far. Just right.

And nobody pestered us for ages. At least thirty minutes!

It was the best cure for grumpiness in the whole wide world.

Is a golden retriever the dog for you?

Hi! It's me, Alfreeda!

I HAVE to set one thing straight: many golden retrievers aren't at all like Gracie! They're calm, friendly and really gentle. So perhaps you'd like your own beautiful golden retriever now. I don't blame you. Retrievers are great pets for families! That is, most families. But before you run off to buy or adopt one, here are some important facts you should know:

Retrievers are large dogs that need lots of exercise. If you live in a little flat, get a little dog instead. And if you can't promise to take your dog on a walk every day, don't get a dog at all. Get a goldfish.

Retrievers moult. That means that some of their hair falls out sometimes. Their waterproof topcoat moults a little bit throughout the year. Their soft undercoat (which keeps them cool in the summer and warm in the winter), moults in the spring and autumn. If your family doesn't like dog hair on the sofa or rugs, get a dog that doesn't moult, like a West Highland terrier.

Retrievers are crepuscular. That means they're more active when the sun rises and the sun sets. They sleep more in the middle of the day. If people in your family like to lie-in, or don't like being pestered at bedtime, it might be better not to get a retriever! (Because a tired family is a grumpy family!)

Okay, signing off for now ... until the next adventure at Hound Hotel!

Yours very factually,

Alfreeda Wolfe

Glossary

admit agree that something is true, often against your wishes

bruise dark mark you get on your skin when you fall or are hit by something

demand claim something or ask for something firmly

guest person or animal who is staying in a hotel

human a person

impressive having the power to impress; to have an effect on someone's thoughts or feelings

interrupt start talking before someone else has finished talking

serious sincere and not funny

shriek cry out or scream in a shrill, piercing way

whistle high, shrill sound made by blowing air through the lips

wilderness area of wild land where no people live

Talk about it

1. Why do you think it is easier for siblings to get along when they are adults than when they are children?

2. What important facts about working with dogs did Alfreeda remember that Alfie forgot?

3. On page 68, Alfreeda has shared some facts (and opinions) about golden retrievers. Do you think a golden retriever would be a good dog for your family? Why or why not?

Write about it

1. Because Hound Hotel has become so busy, Winifred needs someone else to help out. Write a help-wanted advertisement. Make sure you include all the skills someone would need. What type of experience and attitude would also be helpful?

2. This story has quite a few grumpy characters. Write your own short story with at least one bad-tempered character.

3. Research pugs and golden retrievers. Then write a list of things that are similar and different about the two dogs.

About the author

Shelley Swanson Sateren grew up with five pet dogs —
a beagle, a terrier mix, a terrier-poodle mix, a
Weimaraner and a German shorthaired pointer. As an
adult, she adopted a lively West Highland white terrier
called Max. Apart from writing many children's books,
Shelley has worked as a children's book editor and in a
children's bookshop. She lives in Minnesota, USA, with
her husband, and has two grown-up sons.

About the illustrator

Deborah Melmon has worked as an illustrator for
over 25 years. After graduating from the Academy of
Art University in San Francisco, she began her career
illustrating covers for a weekly magazine supplement
newspaper. Since then, she has produced artwork for over
twenty children's books. Her artwork can also be found
on wrapping paper, greeting cards and fabric. Deborah
lives in California, USA, and shares her studio with an
energetic Airedale terrier called Mack.